KARATE Journal SECTIONS

01 **Karate Goals**

Write down your goals for this year

02 **Training Logbook**

Record your training sessions and details

03 **Tournament Logbook**

Write further details of your Tournaments to keep a record for future reference

04 **Instructor Feedback**

Improvements suggested by your Instructor

05 **Autographs & Photos**

Gather the autographs and photos from Tournaments

©The Life Graduate Publishing Group

No part of this book may be scanned, reproduced or distributed in any printed or electronic form without the prior permission of the author or publisher.

KARATE
Journal

Name _____

Age _____

Year _____

Division _____

Dojo _____

Karate Journal

Your Current Belt

Color in your current belt level

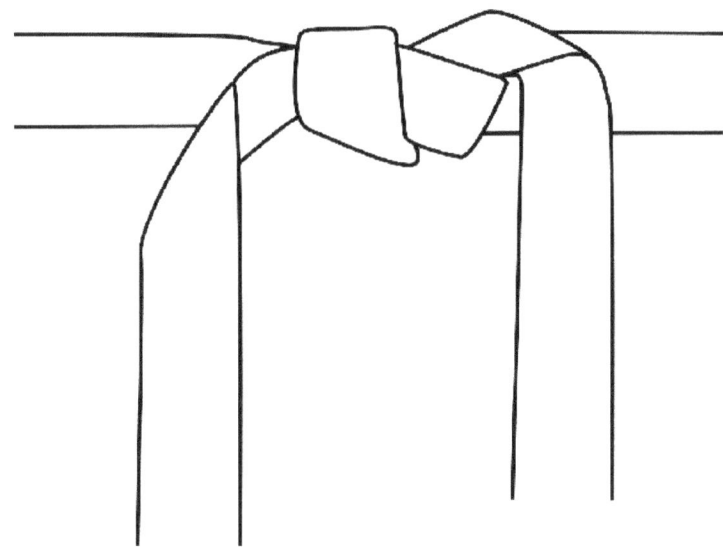

Color and update your belt levels during the year

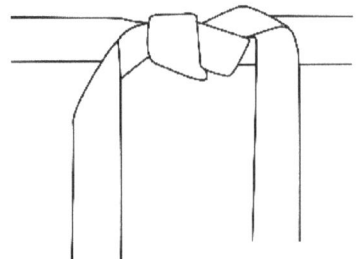 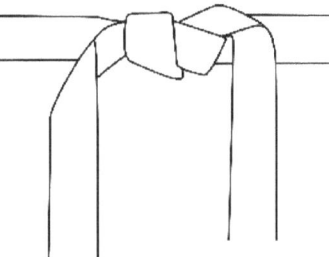 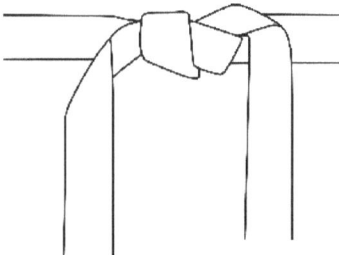

-Karate-

01

KARATE GOALS

01
KARATE TRAINING GOALS

GOAL 1 ....
....
....

GOAL 2 ....
....
....

GOAL 3 ....
....
....

KARATE TOURNAMENT GOALS

GOAL 1 ....

GOAL 2 ....

GOAL 3 ....

02

TRAINING LOGBOOK

TRAINING

Date: /   /   **Start time**   :

End time   :

Skills Completed   Write down the skills you worked on and developed during your class.

....
....
....
....

Skills to improve   Write down areas that you can improve on for your next training session.

....
....
....
....

Instructor Feedback   Write down if your Instructor has a skill, technique or combination for you to focus on.

....
....

Extra Notes   Do you have additional notes or thoughts you would like to write down?

....
....
....

TRAINING

Date: / /   **Start time** :

End time :

Skills Completed   Write down the skills you worked on and developed during your class.

....
....
....
....

Skills to improve   Write down areas that you can improve on for your next training session.

....
....
....
....

Instructor Feedback   Write down if your Instructor has a skill, technique or combination for you to focus on.

....
....

Extra Notes   Do you have additional notes or thoughts you would like to write down?

....
....
....

TRAINING

Date: / / **Start time** :

End time :

Skills Completed Write down the skills you worked on and developed during your class.

....
....
....
....

Skills to improve Write down areas that you can improve on for your next training session.

....
....
....
....

Instructor Feedback Write down if your Instructor has a skill, technique or combination for you to focus on.

....
....

Extra Notes Do you have additional notes or thoughts you would like to write down?

....
....
....

TRAINING

Date: / /   **Start time** :

End time :

Skills Completed
Write down the skills you worked on and developed during your class.

....
....
....
....

Skills to improve
Write down areas that you can improve on for your next training session.

....
....
....
....

Instructor Feedback
Write down if your Instructor has a skill, technique or combination for you to focus on.

....
....

Extra Notes
Do you have additional notes or thoughts you would like to write down?

....
....
....

TRAINING

Date: / /   **Start time**   :

End time   :

Skills Completed   Write down the skills you worked on and developed during your class.

....
....
....
....

Skills to improve   Write down areas that you can improve on for your next training session.

....
....
....
....

Instructor Feedback   Write down if your Instructor has a skill, technique or combination for you to focus on.

....
....

Extra Notes   Do you have additional notes or thoughts you would like to write down?

....
....
....

TRAINING

Date: / /   **Start time** :

End time :

Skills Completed
Write down the skills you worked on and developed during your class.

....
....
....
....

Skills to improve
Write down areas that you can improve on for your next training session.

....
....
....
....

Instructor Feedback
Write down if your Instructor has a skill, technique or combination for you to focus on.

....
....

Extra Notes
Do you have additional notes or thoughts you would like to write down?

....
....
....

TRAINING

Date: / /   **Start time** :

End time :

Skills Completed
Write down the skills you worked on and developed during your class.

....
....
....
....

Skills to improve
Write down areas that you can improve on for your next training session.

....
....
....
....

Instructor Feedback
Write down if your Instructor has a skill, technique or combination for you to focus on.

....
....

Extra Notes
Do you have additional notes or thoughts you would like to write down?

....
....
....

TRAINING

Date: / /   **Start time**   :

End time   :

Skills Completed
Write down the skills you worked on and developed during your class.

....
....
....
....

Skills to improve
Write down areas that you can improve on for your next training session.

....
....
....
....

Instructor Feedback
Write down if your Instructor has a skill, technique or combination for you to focus on.

....
....

Extra Notes
Do you have additional notes or thoughts you would like to write down?

....
....
....

TRAINING

Date: / /   **Start time** :

End time :

Skills Completed
Write down the skills you worked on and developed during your class.

....
....
....
....

Skills to improve
Write down areas that you can improve on for your next training session.

....
....
....
....

Instructor Feedback
Write down if your Instructor has a skill, technique or combination for you to focus on.

....
....

Extra Notes
Do you have additional notes or thoughts you would like to write down?

....
....
....

TRAINING

Date: / /   **Start time** :

End time :

Skills Completed
Write down the skills you worked on and developed during your class.

....
....
....
....

Skills to improve
Write down areas that you can improve on for your next training session.

....
....
....
....

Instructor Feedback
Write down if your Instructor has a skill, technique or combination for you to focus on.

....
....

Extra Notes
Do you have additional notes or thoughts you would like to write down?

....
....
....

TRAINING

Date: / /   **Start time** :

End time :

Skills Completed Write down the skills you worked on and developed during your class.

....
....
....
....

Skills to improve Write down areas that you can improve on for your next training session.

....
....
....

Instructor Feedback Write down if your Instructor has a skill, technique or combination for you to focus on.

....
....

Extra Notes Do you have additional notes or thoughts you would like to write down?

....
....
....

TRAINING

Date: / /   **Start time** :

End time :

Skills Completed
Write down the skills you worked on and developed during your class.

....
....
....
....

Skills to improve
Write down areas that you can improve on for your next training session.

....
....
....
....

Instructor Feedback
Write down if your Instructor has a skill, technique or combination for you to focus on.

....
....

Extra Notes
Do you have additional notes or thoughts you would like to write down?

....
....
....

TRAINING

Date: / /

Start time :

End time :

Skills Completed
Write down the skills you worked on and developed during your class.

....
....
....
....

Skills to improve
Write down areas that you can improve on for your next training session.

....
....
....
....

Instructor Feedback
Write down if your Instructor has a skill, technique or combination for you to focus on.

....
....

Extra Notes
Do you have additional notes or thoughts you would like to write down?

....
....
....

TRAINING

Date: / /   **Start time**   :

End time   :

Skills Completed   Write down the skills you worked on and developed during your class.

....
....
....
....

Skills to improve   Write down areas that you can improve on for your next training session.

....
....
....
....

Instructor Feedback   Write down if your Instructor has a skill, technique or combination for you to focus on.

....
....

Extra Notes   Do you have additional notes or thoughts you would like to write down?

....
....
....

TRAINING

Date: / /   **Start time** :

End time :

Skills Completed
Write down the skills you worked on and developed during your class.

....
....
....
....

Skills to improve
Write down areas that you can improve on for your next training session.

....
....
....
....

Instructor Feedback
Write down if your Instructor has a skill, technique or combination for you to focus on.

....
....

Extra Notes
Do you have additional notes or thoughts you would like to write down?

....
....
....

TRAINING

Date: / /   **Start time** :

                          End time :

Skills Completed
Write down the skills you worked on and developed during your class.

....
....
....
....

Skills to improve
Write down areas that you can improve on for your next training session.

....
....
....
....

Instructor Feedback
Write down if your Instructor has a skill, technique or combination for you to focus on.

....
....

Extra Notes
Do you have additional notes or thoughts you would like to write down?

....
....
....

TRAINING

Date: /   /   **Start time**   :

End time   :

Skills Completed   Write down the skills you worked on and developed during your class.

....
....
....
....

Skills to improve   Write down areas that you can improve on for your next training session.

....
....
....
....

Instructor Feedback   Write down if your Instructor has a skill, technique or combination for you to focus on.

....
....

Extra Notes   Do you have additional notes or thoughts you would like to write down?

....
....
....

TRAINING

Date: / / **Start time** :

End time :

Skills Completed
Write down the skills you worked on and developed during your class.

....
....
....
....

Skills to improve
Write down areas that you can improve on for your next training session.

....
....
....
....

Instructor Feedback
Write down if your Instructor has a skill, technique or combination for you to focus on.

....
....

Extra Notes
Do you have additional notes or thoughts you would like to write down?

....
....
....

TRAINING

Date: / /   **Start time** :

End time :

Skills Completed
Write down the skills you worked on and developed during your class.

....
....
....
....

Skills to improve
Write down areas that you can improve on for your next training session.

....
....
....
....

Instructor Feedback
Write down if your Instructor has a skill, technique or combination for you to focus on.

....
....

Extra Notes
Do you have additional notes or thoughts you would like to write down?

....
....
....

TRAINING

Date: / /   **Start time** :

End time :

Skills Completed   Write down the skills you worked on and developed during your class.

....
....
....
....

Skills to improve   Write down areas that you can improve on for your next training session.

....
....
....
....

Instructor Feedback   Write down if your Instructor has a skill, technique or combination for you to focus on.

....
....

Extra Notes   Do you have additional notes or thoughts you would like to write down?

....
....
....

TRAINING

Date: /   /   **Start time**   :

End time   :

Skills Completed
Write down the skills you worked on and developed during your class.

....
....
....
....

Skills to improve
Write down areas that you can improve on for your next training session.

....
....
....
....

Instructor Feedback
Write down if your Instructor has a skill, technique or combination for you to focus on.

....
....

Extra Notes
Do you have additional notes or thoughts you would like to write down?

....
....
....

TRAINING

Date: / /

Start time :

End time :

Skills Completed
Write down the skills you worked on and developed during your class.

....
....
....
....

Skills to improve
Write down areas that you can improve on for your next training session.

....
....
....
....

Instructor Feedback
Write down if your Instructor has a skill, technique or combination for you to focus on.

....
....

Extra Notes
Do you have additional notes or thoughts you would like to write down?

....
....
....

TRAINING

Date: / / **Start time** :

End time :

Skills Completed Write down the skills you worked on and developed during your class.

....
....
....
....

Skills to improve Write down areas that you can improve on for your next training session.

....
....
....
....

Instructor Feedback Write down if your Instructor has a skill, technique or combination for you to focus on.

....
....

Extra Notes Do you have additional notes or thoughts you would like to write down?

....
....
....

TRAINING

Date: / /   **Start time** :

End time :

Skills Completed
Write down the skills you worked on and developed during your class.

....
....
....
....

Skills to improve
Write down areas that you can improve on for your next training session.

....
....
....
....

Instructor Feedback
Write down if your Instructor has a skill, technique or combination for you to focus on.

....
....

Extra Notes
Do you have additional notes or thoughts you would like to write down?

....
....
....

TRAINING

Date: / /

Start time :

End time :

Skills Completed
Write down the skills you worked on and developed during your class.

....
....
....
....

Skills to improve
Write down areas that you can improve on for your next training session.

....
....
....
....

Instructor Feedback
Write down if your Instructor has a skill, technique or combination for you to focus on.

....
....

Extra Notes
Do you have additional notes or thoughts you would like to write down?

....
....
....

TRAINING

Date: / /   **Start time** :

End time :

Skills Completed
Write down the skills you worked on and developed during your class.

....
....
....
....

Skills to improve
Write down areas that you can improve on for your next training session.

....
....
....
....

Instructor Feedback
Write down if your Instructor has a skill, technique or combination for you to focus on.

....
....

Extra Notes
Do you have additional notes or thoughts you would like to write down?

....
....
....

TRAINING

Date: / /   **Start time** :

End time :

Skills Completed
Write down the skills you worked on and developed during your class.

....
....
....
....

Skills to improve
Write down areas that you can improve on for your next training session.

....
....
....
....

Instructor Feedback
Write down if your Instructor has a skill, technique or combination for you to focus on.

....
....

Extra Notes
Do you have additional notes or thoughts you would like to write down?

....
....
....

TRAINING

Date: / / **Start time** :

End time :

Skills Completed
Write down the skills you worked on and developed during your class.

....
....
....
....

Skills to improve
Write down areas that you can improve on for your next training session.

....
....
....
....

Instructor Feedback
Write down if your Instructor has a skill, technique or combination for you to focus on.

....
....

Extra Notes
Do you have additional notes or thoughts you would like to write down?

....
....
....

TRAINING

Date: /   /   Start time   :

End time   :

Skills Completed
Write down the skills you worked on and developed during your class.

....
....
....
....

Skills to improve
Write down areas that you can improve on for your next training session.

....
....
....
....

Instructor Feedback
Write down if your Instructor has a skill, technique or combination for you to focus on.

....
....

Extra Notes
Do you have additional notes or thoughts you would like to write down?

....
....
....

TRAINING

Date: / /   **Start time** :

End time :

Skills Completed
Write down the skills you worked on and developed during your class.

....
....
....
....

Skills to improve
Write down areas that you can improve on for your next training session.

....
....
....
....

Instructor Feedback
Write down if your Instructor has a skill, technique or combination for you to focus on.

....
....

Extra Notes
Do you have additional notes or thoughts you would like to write down?

....
....
....

TRAINING

Date: / / **Start time** :

End time :

Skills Completed Write down the skills you worked on and developed during your class.

....
....
....
....

Skills to improve Write down areas that you can improve on for your next training session.

....
....
....
....

Instructor Feedback Write down if your Instructor has a skill, technique or combination for you to focus on.

....
....

Extra Notes Do you have additional notes or thoughts you would like to write down?

....
....
....

TRAINING

Date: / / **Start time** :

End time :

Skills Completed
Write down the skills you worked on and developed during your class.

....
....
....
....

Skills to improve
Write down areas that you can improve on for your next training session.

....
....
....
....

Instructor Feedback
Write down if your Instructor has a skill, technique or combination for you to focus on.

....
....

Extra Notes
Do you have additional notes or thoughts you would like to write down?

....
....
....

TRAINING

Date: / / **Start time** :

End time :

Skills Completed Write down the skills you worked on and developed during your class.

....
....
....
....

Skills to improve Write down areas that you can improve on for your next training session.

....
....
....
....

Instructor Feedback Write down if your Instructor has a skill, technique or combination for you to focus on.

....
....

Extra Notes Do you have additional notes or thoughts you would like to write down?

....
....
....

TRAINING

Date: / / **Start time** :

End time :

Skills Completed
Write down the skills you worked on and developed during your class.

....
....
....
....

Skills to improve
Write down areas that you can improve on for your next training session.

....
....
....
....

Instructor Feedback
Write down if your Instructor has a skill, technique or combination for you to focus on.

....
....

Extra Notes
Do you have additional notes or thoughts you would like to write down?

....
....
....

TRAINING

Date: / / **Start time** :
              End time :

Skills Completed Write down the skills you worked on and developed during your class.

....
....
....
....

Skills to improve Write down areas that you can improve on for your next training session.

....
....
....
....

Instructor Feedback Write down if your Instructor has a skill, technique or combination for you to focus on.

....
....

Extra Notes Do you have additional notes or thoughts you would like to write down?

....
....
....

TRAINING

Date: / / **Start time** :

End time :

Skills Completed
Write down the skills you worked on and developed during your class.

....
....
....
....

Skills to improve
Write down areas that you can improve on for your next training session.

....
....
....
....

Instructor Feedback
Write down if your Instructor has a skill, technique or combination for you to focus on.

....
....

Extra Notes
Do you have additional notes or thoughts you would like to write down?

....
....
....

TRAINING

Date: / / **Start time** :

End time :

Skills Completed
Write down the skills you worked on and developed during your class.

....

....

....

....

Skills to improve
Write down areas that you can improve on for your next training session.

....

....

....

....

Instructor Feedback
Write down if your Instructor has a skill, technique or combination for you to focus on.

....

....

Extra Notes
Do you have additional notes or thoughts you would like to write down?

....

....

....

TRAINING

Date: / / **Start time** :

End time :

Skills Completed
Write down the skills you worked on and developed during your class.

....
....
....
....

Skills to improve
Write down areas that you can improve on for your next training session.

....
....
....
....

Instructor Feedback
Write down if your Instructor has a skill, technique or combination for you to focus on.

....
....

Extra Notes
Do you have additional notes or thoughts you would like to write down?

....
....
....

TRAINING

Date: / /   **Start time** :

End time :

Skills Completed
Write down the skills you worked on and developed during your class.

....
....
....
....

Skills to improve
Write down areas that you can improve on for your next training session.

....
....
....
....

Instructor Feedback
Write down if your Instructor has a skill, technique or combination for you to focus on.

....
....

Extra Notes
Do you have additional notes or thoughts you would like to write down?

....
....
....

TRAINING

Date: / /   **Start time** :

End time :

Skills Completed
Write down the skills you worked on and developed during your class.

....
....
....
....

Skills to improve
Write down areas that you can improve on for your next training session.

....
....
....
....

Instructor Feedback
Write down if your Instructor has a skill, technique or combination for you to focus on.

....
....

Extra Notes
Do you have additional notes or thoughts you would like to write down?

....
....
....

TRAINING

Date: / /   **Start time** :

End time :

Skills Completed
Write down the skills you worked on and developed during your class.

....
....
....
....

Skills to improve
Write down areas that you can improve on for your next training session.

....
....
....
....

Instructor Feedback
Write down if your Instructor has a skill, technique or combination for you to focus on.

....
....

Extra Notes
Do you have additional notes or thoughts you would like to write down?

....
....
....

TRAINING

Date: / /   **Start time**   :

End time   :

Skills Completed
Write down the skills you worked on and developed during your class.

....
....
....
....

Skills to improve
Write down areas that you can improve on for your next training session.

....
....
....
....

Instructor Feedback
Write down if your Instructor has a skill, technique or combination for you to focus on.

....
....

Extra Notes
Do you have additional notes or thoughts you would like to write down?

....
....
....

TRAINING

Date: / / **Start time** :

End time :

Skills Completed
Write down the skills you worked on and developed during your class.

....
....
....
....

Skills to improve
Write down areas that you can improve on for your next training session.

....
....
....
....

Instructor Feedback
Write down if your Instructor has a skill, technique or combination for you to focus on.

....
....

Extra Notes
Do you have additional notes or thoughts you would like to write down?

....
....
....

TRAINING

Date: / / **Start time** :

End time :

Skills Completed
Write down the skills you worked on and developed during your class.

....
....
....
....

Skills to improve
Write down areas that you can improve on for your next training session.

....
....
....
....

Instructor Feedback
Write down if your Instructor has a skill, technique or combination for you to focus on.

....
....

Extra Notes
Do you have additional notes or thoughts you would like to write down?

....
....
....

TRAINING

Date: /   /   **Start time**   :

End time   :

Skills Completed
Write down the skills you worked on and developed during your class.

....
....
....
....

Skills to improve
Write down areas that you can improve on for your next training session.

....
....
....
....

Instructor Feedback
Write down if your Instructor has a skill, technique or combination for you to focus on.

....
....

Extra Notes
Do you have additional notes or thoughts you would like to write down?

....
....
....

TRAINING

Date: / /   **Start time** :

End time :

Skills Completed   Write down the skills you worked on and developed during your class.

....
....
....
....

Skills to improve   Write down areas that you can improve on for your next training session.

....
....
....
....

Instructor Feedback   Write down if your Instructor has a skill, technique or combination for you to focus on.

....
....

Extra Notes   Do you have additional notes or thoughts you would like to write down?

....
....
....

TRAINING

Date: / / **Start time** :

End time :

Skills Completed
Write down the skills you worked on and developed during your class.

....
....
....
....

Skills to improve
Write down areas that you can improve on for your next training session.

....
....
....
....

Instructor Feedback
Write down if your Instructor has a skill, technique or combination for you to focus on.

....
....

Extra Notes
Do you have additional notes or thoughts you would like to write down?

....
....
....

TRAINING

Date: / / **Start time** :
 End time :

Skills Completed
Write down the skills you worked on and developed during your class.

....
....
....
....

Skills to improve
Write down areas that you can improve on for your next training session.

....
....
....
....

Instructor Feedback
Write down if your Instructor has a skill, technique or combination for you to focus on.

....
....

Extra Notes
Do you have additional notes or thoughts you would like to write down?

....
....
....

TRAINING

Date: / / **Start time** :

End time :

Skills Completed
Write down the skills you worked on and developed during your class.

....
....
....
....

Skills to improve
Write down areas that you can improve on for your next training session.

....
....
....
....

Instructor Feedback
Write down if your Instructor has a skill, technique or combination for you to focus on.

....
....

Extra Notes
Do you have additional notes or thoughts you would like to write down?

....
....
....

TRAINING

Date: / / **Start time** :

End time :

Skills Completed
Write down the skills you worked on and developed during your class.

....
....
....
....

Skills to improve
Write down areas that you can improve on for your next training session.

....
....
....
....

Instructor Feedback
Write down if your Instructor has a skill, technique or combination for you to focus on.

....
....

Extra Notes
Do you have additional notes or thoughts you would like to write down?

....
....
....

TRAINING

Date: / / **Start time** :

End time :

Skills Completed
Write down the skills you worked on and developed during your class.

....
....
....
....

Skills to improve
Write down areas that you can improve on for your next training session.

....
....
....
....

Instructor Feedback
Write down if your Instructor has a skill, technique or combination for you to focus on.

....
....

Extra Notes
Do you have additional notes or thoughts you would like to write down?

....
....
....

03
TOURNAMENT LOGBOOK

TOURNAMENT DAY

Date: / /   **Start time**   :

Location: ....

Details of Tournament
(eg. Points Awarded, Division Outcome etc.)

Instructor Feedback

....
....
....

My Performance — Write down how you felt you contributed to the Tournament. Did the Instructor provide you with any personal feedback? Did you have any highlights? Do you have areas to improve on?

....
....
....
....

TOURNAMENT DAY

Date: /   /   **Start time**   :

Location: ....

Details of Tournament
(eg. Points Awarded, Division Outcome etc.)

Instructor Feedback

....
....
....

My Performance — Write down how you felt you contributed to the Tournament. Did the Instructor provide you with any personal feedback? Did you have any highlights? Do you have areas to improve on?

....
....
....
....

TOURNAMENT DAY

Date: /   /   **Start time**   :

Location: ....

Details of Tournament
(eg. Points Awarded, Division Outcome etc.)

Instructor Feedback

....
....
....

My Performance   Write down how you felt you contributed to the Tournament. Did the Instructor provide you with any personal feedback? Did you have any highlights? Do you have areas to improve on?

....
....
....
....

TOURNAMENT DAY

Date: / /   **Start time** :

Location: ....

Details of Tournament
(eg. Points Awarded, Division Outcome etc.)

Instructor Feedback

....
....
....

My Performance — Write down how you felt you contributed to the Tournament. Did the Instructor provide you with any personal feedback? Did you have any highlights? Do you have areas to improve on?

....
....
....
....

TOURNAMENT DAY

Date: /   /   **Start time**   :

Location: ....

Details of Tournament
(eg. Points Awarded, Division Outcome etc.)

Instructor Feedback

....
....
....

My Performance Write down how you felt you contributed to the Tournament. Did the Instructor provide you with any personal feedback? Did you have any highlights? Do you have areas to improve on?

....
....
....
....

TOURNAMENT DAY

Date: /   /   **Start time**   :

Location: ....

Details of Tournament
(eg. Points Awarded, Division Outcome etc.)

Instructor Feedback

....
....
....

My Performance Write down how you felt you contributed to the Tournament. Did the Instructor provide you with any personal feedback? Did you have any highlights? Do you have areas to improve on?

....
....
....
....

TOURNAMENT DAY

Date: / /   **Start time** :

Location: ....

Details of Tournament
(eg. Points Awarded, Division Outcome etc.)

Instructor Feedback

....
....
....

My Performance Write down how you felt you contributed to the Tournament. Did the Instructor provide you with any personal feedback? Did you have any highlights? Do you have areas to improve on?

....
....
....
....

TOURNAMENT DAY

Date: /   /   **Start time**   :

Location: ....

Details of Tournament
(eg. Points Awarded, Division Outcome etc.)

Instructor Feedback

....
....
....

My Performance

Write down how you felt you contributed to the Tournament. Did the Instructor provide you with any personal feedback? Did you have any highlights? Do you have areas to improve on?

....
....
....
....

TOURNAMENT DAY

Date: /   /   **Start time**   :

Location: ....

Details of Tournament
(eg. Points Awarded, Division Outcome etc.)

Instructor Feedback

....
....
....

My Performance   Write down how you felt you contributed to the Tournament. Did the Instructor provide you with any personal feedback? Did you have any highlights? Do you have areas to improve on?

....
....
....
....

TOURNAMENT DAY

Date: / /   **Start time** :

Location: ....

Details of Tournament
(eg. Points Awarded, Division Outcome etc.)

Instructor Feedback

....
....
....

My Performance — Write down how you felt you contributed to the Tournament. Did the Instructor provide you with any personal feedback? Did you have any highlights? Do you have areas to improve on?

....
....
....
....

TOURNAMENT DAY

Date: / /   **Start time** :

Location: ....

Details of Tournament
(eg. Points Awarded, Division Outcome etc.)

Instructor Feedback

....
....
....

My Performance — Write down how you felt you contributed to the Tournament. Did the Instructor provide you with any personal feedback? Did you have any highlights? Do you have areas to improve on?

....
....
....
....

04

INSTRUCTOR NOTES

NOTES

NOTES

NOTES

05

Autographs & Photos

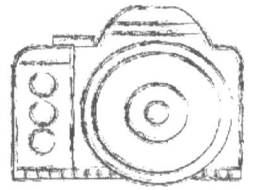

Autographs & Photo's

Autographs & Photo's

Autographs & Photo's

Autographs & Photo's

Autographs & Photo's

KARATE
Journal

The Life Graduate
PUBLISHING GROUP

-Karate-